# Itsy-Bitsy Cloud
## A Secret Wish Granted

The Screenplay

Francis Edwards

Ukiyoto Publishing

All global publishing rights are held by

**Ukiyoto Publishing**

Published in 2023

Content Copyright © Francis Edwards

**ISBN 9789359205144**

All rights reserved.
No part of this publication may be reproduced, transmitted, or stored in a retrieval system, in any form by any means, electronic, mechanical, photocopying, recording or otherwise, without the prior permission of the publisher.

The moral rights of the author have been asserted.

This is a work of fiction. Names, characters, businesses, places, events, locales, and incidents are either the products of the author's imagination or used in a fictitious manner. Any resemblance to actual persons, living or dead, or actual events is purely coincidental.

This book is sold subject to the condition that it shall not by way of trade or otherwise, be lent, resold, hired out or otherwise circulated, without the publisher's prior consent, in any form of binding or cover other than that in which it is published.

www.ukiyoto.com

# Contents

| | |
|---|---|
| ACT 1 - Itsy – Bitsy's Secret | 1 |
| ACT 2 - Itsy – Bitsy Writes A Poem | 6 |
| ACT 3 - Itsy – Bitsy's Tells Her Secret | 12 |
| ACT 4 - The Deep Dream | 17 |
| ACT 5 - Visit With The Brownies | 23 |
| ACT 6 - The Apple Tree Fairy Chieftain | 30 |
| ACT 7 - Leprechauns | 36 |
| ACT 8 - War Of The Gnomes | 40 |
| ACT 9 - The Elves | 45 |
| ACT 10 - Chain Link | 50 |
| ACT 11 - Kelpie, The Horse | 54 |
| ACT 12 - The Storm | 56 |

# ACT 1 -Itsy – Bitsy's Secret

Setting: A quaint town with a small house, school, and playground

          INT. ITSY-BITSY'S BEDROOM - MORNING

A soft sunbeam filters through the curtains, illuminating Itsy-Bitsy's room. Itsy-Bitsy, a curious and imaginative little girl, lies in bed with a content smile on her face.

NARRATOR (V.O.)
Once upon a time, in a quaint town, lived a little girl named Itsy-Bitsy. She had a wonderful spirit and a secret wish.

ItsBitsy looks out of her window, her eyes fixed on the sky.

          EXT. PLAYGROUND - DAY

Itsy-Bitsy walks towards the playground, lost in thought, when her older brother ZIGGY, a typical mischievous sibling, catches up with her.

ZIGGY
Hey, Itsy-Bitsy, what are you daydreaming about this time?

ITSY-BITSY
(brushing off)
Oh, nothing, Ziggy.

ZIGGY
(grinning)
Come on, tell me! I won't laugh, I promise.

Itsy-Bitsy hesitates for a moment, then leans closer to Ziggy.

ITSY-BITSY
(whispering)
I want to climb on a cloud.

ZIGGY
(bursts into laughter)
Climb on a cloud? Seriously?

Itsy-Bitsy rolls her eyes and walks away, leaving Ziggy laughing behind her.

INT. CLASSROOM - DAY

Itsy-Bitsy sits at her assigned window seat, gazing out at the passing clouds. Her TEACHER, a kind woman, walks by.

TEACHER
(leaning down)
Itsy-Bitsy, are you paying attention?

ITSY-BITSY
(smiling)
Yes, Miss. Just taking a little break.

TEACHER
(chuckles)
Alright, but remember, we need to focus on our studies too.

Itsy-Bitsy nods, still glancing at the clouds outside.

EXT. SCHOOL PLAYGROUND - DAY

During recess, Itsy-Bitsy's friends chat and play, but Itsy-Bitsy sits under a tree with her diary, sketching clouds and shapes.

NARRATOR (V.O.)
Itsy-Bitsy loved clouds, especially the way they changed shape before disappearing into the horizon.

Her friends exchange curious glances but continue with their games.

INT. KITCHEN - EVENING

Itsy-Bitsy's mother, MERRY-WEATHER, speaks to other mothers about Itsy-Bitsy's fascination with clouds at the playground.

MERRY-WEATHER
(sighs)
She's always looking up, you know? I don't understand it.

OTHER MOTHER
(smiling)
Kids and their quirks! As long as she's happy.

INT. ITSY-BITSY'S BEDROOM - NIGHT

Itsy-Bitsy flips through her diary, filled with cloud sketches. She smiles and writes about the different shapes she's imagined.

NARRATOR (V.O.)
Every day, Itsy-Bitsy would draw clouds and imagine them as ships, animals, stars, and more.

She closes the diary with a content sigh.

EXT. FRONT YARD - DAY

Itsy-Bitsy shows her latest cloud drawing to her father, STORM, who studies it with genuine interest.

STORM
(grinning)
Your clouds are always the highlight of your drawings, Itsy-Bitsy. You have a special way with them.

ITSY-BITSY
(blushing)
Thanks, Dad.

INT. SCIENCE CLASSROOM - DAY

Itsy-Bitsy's science teacher explains different cloud formations to the class.

TEACHER
(pointing to diagrams)
These are the high clouds, the middle clouds, and the low clouds.

Itsy-Bitsy takes diligent notes, her eyes shining with excitement.

```
ITSY-BITSY
(to herself)
There's so much more to learn about clouds.
```

# ACT 2 - Itsy – Bitsy Writes A Poem

Setting: Itsy-Bitsy's home, school, and playground

INT. ITSY-BITSY'S BEDROOM - MORNING

Itsy-Bitsy sits at her desk, notebook open in front of her. She glances outside her window and spots a cirrus cloud.

NARRATOR (V.O.)

Itsy-Bitsy's fascination with clouds now helps her predict the weather. No more teasing from Ziggy.

EXT. PLAYGROUND - DAY

Itsy-Bitsy walks towards the playground when her friends approach her, eager to know the weather.

FRIEND 1

(excited)

Hey, Itsy-Bitsy! What's the weather going to be like tomorrow?

ITSY-BITSY

(smiling)

Tomorrow? I'd say pack an umbrella, just in case.

Her friends laugh and thank her.

INT. SCHOOL CLASSROOM - DAY

Itsy-Bitsy sits next to a classmate, helping him with his science homework on clouds.

CLASSMATE

(grateful)

Thanks, Itsy-Bitsy. You're a lifesaver.

EXT. SCHOOL GROUNDS - DAY

Mothers approach Itsy-Bitsy, seeking her weather insights.

MOTHER 1

(anxious)

We're planning a picnic this weekend. What's the forecast?

ITSY-BITSY

(smiling)

You're in luck! Sunshine and blue skies all the way.

INT. ITSY-BITSY'S ROOM - NIGHT

Itsy-Bitsy sits at her desk, penning a poem in her diary.

NARRATOR (V.O.)

Itsy-Bitsy's passion for clouds led her to write a special poem, capturing her longing to soar among them.

She finishes writing the poem and reads it to herself.

ITSY-BITSY

(whispering)

"CLOUD, CLOUD, CLOUD... Come down... Could I... Climb aboard."

INT. LIVING ROOM - NIGHT

Itsy-Bitsy enters the living room, where Ziggy is watching TV.

ITSY-BITSY

(excited)

Ziggy, listen to this poem I wrote!

ZIGGY

(disinterested)

Oh great, another one of your weird ideas.

Itsy-Bitsy reads the poem aloud, her excitement clear in her voice.

ITSY-BITSY

"Cloud, Cloud, Cloud... Come down... Could I... Climb aboard."

ZIGGY

(laughing)

Climb on a cloud? You're out of your mind!

ITSY-BITSY

(smiling)

It's just a poem, Ziggy. No need to be so serious.

ZIGGY

(mocking)

I'm telling Mom you're being weird again.

ITSY-BITSY

(teasing)

Just make sure you take out the garbage before it rains.

INT. ITSY-BITSY'S BEDROOM - NIGHT

Itsy-Bitsy shows her poem to her father, Storm, who reads it with admiration.

STORM

(grinning)

Wow, you used so many words starting with 'C'. It's impressive.

ITSY-BITSY

(proud)

Thanks, Dad. It's also helping me with my spelling.


STORM

(handing her a dollar)

You deserve this for your clever poem.


NARRATOR (V.O.)

Itsy-Bitsy's creative use of words caught her father's attention and earned her well-deserved praise.

## ACT 3 - Itsy – Bitsy's Tells Her Secret

Setting: Itsy-Bitsy's back garden with flowers, a large rock, and a flower patch; School; Home

EXT. ITSY-BITSY'S BACK GARDEN - MORNING

Itsy-Bitsy stands in the garden, carefully picking wild flowers. Her mother, MERRY-WEATHER, approaches her.

MERRY-WEATHER

(supportive)

The Garden Club will love these flowers, Itsy-Bitsy. Thanks for helping.

Itsy-Bitsy smiles and nods, but her gaze keeps drifting to the sky.

NARRATOR (V.O.)

As Itsy-Bitsy gathers flowers, her eyes can't help but wander to the clouds above.

Itsy-Bitsy stumbles over a rusty garden ornament and picks it up. She examines the ornament, revealing a small, rusty Cupid.

ITSY-BITSY

(amused)

Look at you, Cupid. What's your story?

The Cupid comes to life and speaks.

CUPID

(grateful)

You found me! I've been hidden away for years.

Itsy-Bitsy places the Cupid on a smoother rock, and he explains that he has one last arrow to grant a wish.

CUPID

(whispering)

My arrow can pierce a Garden Fairy's heart. She might grant you a wish.

ITSY-BITSY

(intrigued)

A wish?


The Cupid shoots the arrow, aiming at a disturbance in a purple flower patch.


ITSY-BITSY

(excited)

There's a Garden Fairy over there!


Itsy-Bitsy spots the Garden Fairy flitting among the flowers, her color changing to match the purple blooms.


GARDEN FAIRY

(whispering)

Tell me your secret, for my heart is pierced.


ITSY-BITSY

(whispering)

My secret wish is to climb on a cloud and drift in the sky.

The Garden Fairy reveals that she can't grant wishes but can pass Itsy-Bitsy's wish to her Godmother Cloud, who can.


GARDEN FAIRY

(whispering)

Godmother Cloud's wand has a star attached. She'll come to you in a white cloud gown.


The Garden Fairy warns Itsy-Bitsy not to tell anyone or her wish will be lost. She'll speak to Godmother Cloud when Itsy-Bitsy is in a deep sleep.


GARDEN FAIRY

(whispering)

Remember, don't tell anyone. Not a word.


The Garden Fairy senses someone approaching and quickly hides among the purple flowers.


GARDEN FAIRY

(whispering)

Farewell, dear one.

The Garden Fairy disappears, and Ziggy approaches.

ZIGGY

(impatient)

What's taking you so long, Itsy-Bitsy? Mom needs those flowers now.

ITSY-BITSY

(flustered)

I'm coming, Ziggy.

Itsy-Bitsy hurries off with a bundle of flowers, her heart racing with the secret she now carries.

## ACT 4 - The Deep Dream

Setting: Itsy-Bitsy's bedroom, Fairy Land Mountain, Other World Terrain

    INT. ITSY-BITSY'S BEDROOM - NIGHT

Itsy-Bitsy lies in her bed, unable to sleep, as her secret weighs heavily on her. Her cat, JUMPING-JACK, curls up next to her.

NARRATOR (V.O.)

Itsy-Bitsy's nights were filled with restlessness as she carried her secret wish, unable to share it.

Itsy-Bitsy starts to toss and turn, and Jumping-Jack begins to meow anxiously.

GODMOTHER FAIRY CLOUD

(appearing)

I have come to grant your wish, my dear child.

Itsy-Bitsy's eyes widen as she looks at Godmother Fairy Cloud.

ITSY-BITSY

(astonished)

You're here!

GODMOTHER FAIRY CLOUD

(smiling)

Indeed. You've kept our secret well, and now it's time to fulfill your wish.

NARRATOR (V.O.)

Itsy-Bitsy's deep, dreamless slumber was about to transform into a journey beyond her imagination.

GODMOTHER FAIRY CLOUD

(proudly)

You've passed the test by keeping the secret. Your wish remains intact.

ITSY-BITSY

(excited)

Thank you! But how do I reach the mountain?

GODMOTHER FAIRY CLOUD

(pointing)

There, my dear, atop Fairy Land Mountain.


EXT. FAIRY LAND MOUNTAIN - NIGHT


Itsy-Bitsy and Jumping-Jack stand at the base of Fairy Land Mountain.


GODMOTHER FAIRY CLOUD

(summoning wind)

To the mountain peak, Cap Cloud!


A cloud forms beneath Itsy-Bitsy, lifting her and Jumping-Jack into the air. They land on the mountain's peak.


GODMOTHER FAIRY CLOUD

(weaving magic)

Cap Cloud, take them to the Other World Terrain.


The cloud takes shape, forming a comfortable seat for Itsy-Bitsy and Jumping-Jack.

GODMOTHER FAIRY CLOUD

(whispering)

Remember, your cat will be your guide. Cling onto his back.

Jumping-Jack allows Itsy-Bitsy to saddle him, and they hold onto each other as the Cap Cloud lifts off.

INT. CAP CLOUD - TRAVELING

Itsy-Bitsy and Jumping-Jack travel on the Cap Cloud through the night sky.

ITSY-BITSY

(amazed)

We're really flying!

GODMOTHER FAIRY CLOUD

(v.o.)

Enjoy the journey, dear one.

NARRATOR (V.O.)

As they soar through the sky, Itsy-Bitsy clings tightly to her cat, looking forward to her adventure in the Other World.

EXT. OTHER WORLD TERRAIN - MORNING

The Cap Cloud descends onto an enchanting landscape of vibrant colors. Itsy-Bitsy and Jumping-Jack disembark.

ITSY-BITSY

(whispering)

This place is incredible!

GODMOTHER FAIRY CLOUD

(v.o.)

Give the postcard to the head chieftain. They will guide you.

Itsy-Bitsy approaches a FAIRY CHIEFTAIN and hands over a postcard. The chieftain smiles and nods.

GODMOTHER FAIRY CLOUD

(v.o.)

Each visit confirmed by the postcard will lead you to new adventures.

As Itsy-Bitsy explores the Other World, she realizes that the fairies here are as real as the clouds she admired.

NARRATOR (V.O.)

Itsy-Bitsy's journey has begun, with new landscapes, friends, and challenges awaiting her.

# ACT 5 - Visit With The Brownies

Setting: Farmland Terrain, Pumpkin Patch, Clap Cloud, Halloween Night

      EXT. FARMLAND TERRAIN - DAY

The Clap Cloud drifts over farmland, revealing barns, animals, and a farmhouse below. Itsy-Bitsy and Jumping-Jack marvel at the view.

ITSY-BITSY

(excited)

Is this the first Terrain?

CAP CLOUD

(v.o.)

Yes, make sure to take the Brownies postcard when you leave.

      EXT. FARMLAND TERRAIN - FARMHOUSE - DAY

Itsy-Bitsy and Jumping-Jack arrive on the farm and are greeted by BROWNIE HARD WORKER.

BROWNIE HARD WORKER

(cheerful)

Welcome! We could use an extra hand on the farm.


Its lines are carried with warmth and a mischievous smile.


BROWNIE HARD WORKER

(grinning)

Your cat can make himself comfortable in that pumpkin over there.


The brownie explains the tradition of pumpkin carving and its significance in scaring away spirits.


ITSY-BITSY

(energetic)

I'm ready to help!


Brownie Hard Worker introduces Itsy-Bitsy to BROWNIE FARMLAND TERRAIN HEAD CHIEFTAIN, who is disguised as a scary pumpkin.

BROWNIE HEAD CHIEFTAIN

(ghoulishly)

Welcome, young one. I'm here to protect the farm on Halloween night.

Itsy-Bitsy is too nervous to hand over her postcard.

CAP CLOUD

(v.o.)

Remember, deliver the postcard after you've completed your task.

INT. PUMPKIN PATCH - DAY

Itsy-Bitsy begins carving faces on pumpkins, while Jumping-Jack explores.

BROWNIE HARD WORKER

(approaching)

You're off to a great start! The animals will love these.

The Hard Worker leaves to inform the Farmland Terrain Chieftain about Itsy-Bitsy's arrival.

BROWNIE HARD WORKER

(yelling)

Look, everyone, Itsy-Bitsy Cloud is here to carve pumpkins for us!

The Chieftain emerges from the shadows, still disguised as a scary pumpkin.

BROWNIE HEAD CHIEFTAIN

(spooky voice)

Welcome, child. I'm here to watch over the farm on Halloween night.

Itsy-Bitsy hesitates, unable to hand over her postcard.

CAP CLOUD

(v.o.)

Deliver the postcard in a clever way.

Itsy-Bitsy continues carving pumpkins, struggling to create new faces.

ITSY-BITSY

(to Jumping-Jack)

Let's make some storm cloud faces to scare away the witches.

She carves clouds on the pumpkins, hoping to create an eerie atmosphere.

BROWNIE HARD WORKER

(returning)

You're doing great! Keep it up.

As the sun sets, Itsy-Bitsy comes up with a plan to deliver her postcard.

ITSY-BITSY

(to Jumping-Jack)

Deliver the postcard inside one of the carved pumpkins.

Jumping-Jack places the postcard inside a pumpkin, and Brownie Hard Worker takes it to the Chieftain.

BROWNIE HARD WORKER

(whispering)

The pumpkin's ready for a candle.

As the Chieftain lifts the pumpkin lid, he discovers the postcard.

BROWNIE HEAD CHIEFTAIN

(signing postcard)

Very well done, Itsy-Bitsy Cloud.

The Garden Fairy, now orange, appears and takes the postcard.

      EXT. FARMLAND TERRAIN - HALLOWEEN NIGHT

As Halloween night falls, the Clap Cloud arrives, and Jumping-Jack carries Itsy-Bitsy onto the cloud.

ITSY-BITSY

(grateful)

Thank you, Jumping-Jack.


They ascend onto the Clap Cloud, leaving behind the lighted pumpkins and strange shadows of Halloween night.

## ACT 6 - The Apple Tree Fairy Chieftain

Setting: Dryads Terrain, Enchanted Forest, Apple Tree, Postcard Trick

EXT. DENSE FOREST - DAY

The Clap Cloud hovers over an enchanted forest, and Itsy-Bitsy and Jumping-Jack jump off onto a path between ancient trees.

ITSY-BITSY

(amazed)

Look at these trees, Jumping-Jack. They're so old!

As they continue, Itsy-Bitsy notices knots on the trees resembling faces.

ITSY-BITSY

(curious)

It's like the trees have faces.

Jumping-Jack hisses and becomes tense, refusing to move forward.

ITSY-BITSY

(worried)

What's wrong, Jumping-Jack?

OLD APPLE TREE

(hollow voice)

Welcome to the Dryads Terrain. I am the Chieftain Apple Tree.

Itsy-Bitsy and Jumping-Jack freeze as the tree speaks.

ITSY-BITSY

(nervous)

Wh-who are you?

OLD APPLE TREE

I am the Chieftain Apple Tree. You can call me Apple Tree.

The tree explains the fate of children who lose their postcards or are afraid to approach.

ITSY-BITSY

(to Jumping-Jack, whispering)

Don't worry, we're going to help them.

Itsy-Bitsy gathers postcards from the other children.

ITSY-BITSY

(to the children, whispering)

I have a trick to play on the Chieftain. He won't chase you.

Itsy-Bitsy hides the postcards behind leaves with tree sap.

ITSY-BITSY

(whispering)

Wait for the breeze, then watch the trick.

As the breeze shakes the leaves, the Chieftain reaches for them, discovering the postcards.

ITSY-BITSY

(excited)

Look, children, it worked!

The Garden Fairy, now dressed in green and autumn gold, arrives to collect the postcards.

GARDEN FAIRY

(taking postcards)

Well done, Itsy-Bitsy.

The children celebrate, and Itsy-Bitsy is overjoyed to have new friends.

ITSY-BITSY

(thankful)

Thank you for your help, everyone. We're going to leave together!

The Cap Cloud appears, and Jumping-Jack carries five new friends on his back.

ITSY-BITSY

(happy)

Now we won't be alone on our journey!


As they ascend onto the cloud, Itsy-Bitsy takes a moment to reflect on the Apple Tree.


ITSY-BITSY

(to herself)

A   for Apple, Apple, Apple

Apple Tree...

Able to see red...

Allow to have...

A lot to take.

Away with them...

A good tree...

Account to replace...

Another year will come.

Always a good treat...

Apron on...

Apply good measure...

According to instructions.

Access the...

Aroma to ignite ...

Appetite...

Approval to follow.

Applause...

Allows you another...

Add your blessings for...

Apples, Apples, Apples.

## ACT 7 - Leprechauns

Setting: Leprechaun Terrain, Ireland, Dancing Party, Shoe Trick


EXT. IRISH TERRAIN - DAY


The Clap Cloud carries the children to the Leprechaun Terrain in Ireland. They awaken to the sound of music, dancing, and tapping.


ITSY-BITSY

(excited)

Look, everyone, the Leprechauns are welcoming us with a party!


The children are excited to join the festivities and receive new shoes made by the Leprechaun cobblers.


ITSY-BITSY

(to the Leprechauns)

Thank you so much for the shoes and the warm welcome!

As Itsy-Bitsy talks to the Leprechauns, she notices that they disappear whenever she blinks.

ITSY-BITSY

(to herself)

How can I give the postcards if I keep blinking?

Itsy-Bitsy learns that old shoes are used as fuel for heating the Leprechaun houses.

ITSY-BITSY

(to herself)

Gifts... Leprechauns love gifts!

Itsy-Bitsy secretly gathers the children's postcards and places them in the right shoes. She wraps the shoes and presents them to the Chieftain Leprechaun.

ITSY-BITSY

(to the Chieftain)

Please accept this gift from all of us as a token of our gratitude.

The Chieftain opens the gift, finding the shoes with postcards inside. He signs each postcard, and the Garden Fairy collects them.

ITSY-BITSY

(to the children)

The Cap Cloud is approaching. Let's get ready to leave!

Jumping-Jack, wearing his new blue collar, joins Itsy-Bitsy and the children as they board the Cap Cloud.

ITSY-BITSY

(happy)

We did it! Another adventure and new friends!

As the Cap Cloud takes off, Itsy-Bitsy reflects on their time with the Leprechauns and writes a poem to commemorate the occasion.

B for BOOK, BOOK, BOOK

Believe me, I will read...

Best to enjoy...

Better than playing...

Be my friend.


Becomes my aim to read...

Beyond my knowledge...

Behind my past...

Begin a new adventure.


Brighten any hour...

Becken my thoughts...

Broken my...

Boredom.


Brave little...

Book, Book, Book

Bind the pages...

Bond the story for me.

Believe in Leprechauns.

## ACT 8 - War Of The Gnomes

Setting: Gnome Terrain, Gnome Battle, Truce Celebration

EXT. GNOME TERRAIN - DAY

The Cap Cloud approaches the Gnome Terrain, and Itsy-Bitsy suggests visiting the Gnomes since she knows they're friendly and fun-loving.

CAP CLOUD

Where should we go next in the Other World?

ITSY-BITSY

Let's visit the Gnomes! They're friendly and love to have fun.

The children vote on the destination, and the Gnome Hats win. Itsy-Bitsy is excited since a Green Hat Gnome is holding a sign.

As they land, they discover a battlefield between Red Hat and Green Hat Gnomes.

ITSY-BITSY

(confused)

What's happening here?


A Green Hat Gnome explains that the war began due to humans buying only Red Hat Gnomes, causing jealousy among the Green Hats.


ITSY-BITSY

(to the Gnome)

This needs to be resolved. Let's see if we can help.


The Gnome tells them about the two Gnome Chieftains and the impending battle. The children decide to hide in tree holes to avoid getting involved.


The Chieftain on horseback arrives without a hat, and Itsy-Bitsy collects the postcards from the children.


ITSY-BITSY

(hinting)

You lost your hat?

**CHIEFTAIN GNOME**

(laughing)

No, I took it off to protect myself!

Itsy-Bitsy picks up a red hat and places the postcards inside. The Chieftain puts on the hat, receiving the postcards.

The Red Hat Chieftain announces a truce, and a celebration ensues.

**ITSY-BITSY**

(to the Chieftain)

I'm glad the war is over!

The Garden Fairy, dressed in red and green, collects the postcards and flies off.

The Cap Cloud hovers over the celebration, ready for the children to continue their journey.

H for Hurdle

Heaping on you...
Headed your way...
Hold on.

Have the resolve...
Head for trials...
Hit the target.

Hope for the best...
Hatch another plan...
Hail that one if successful.

Heap that hurdle down...
Hide it behind...
Having another one to face?

Half the list has gone...
Hop to another discovery...
Here comes another secret.

Happy you will be...
Hard not to resist...

Helping others.

Hats of Red...

Hats of Green...

Have your choice...

Home garden will embrace.

## ACT 9 - The Elves

Setting: Santa Kingdom, North Pole, Santa's Workshop, Upcycle Day Festival


EXT. NORTH POLE - DAY


The Cap Cloud heads towards the North Pole, and the children bundle up to keep warm. They spot the reindeer, and the excitement builds.


CHILD 1

(excited)

Look, it's Santa's reindeer!


ITSY-BITSY

(to the children)

Hold on to your hats, it's going to be chilly!


The children arrive at Santa's Kingdom and are greeted by an Elf named Ify. Ify is constantly saying "Ify you do this, Ify I do that." He's very dependent on others.

IFY

(to the children)

If you stand in line, I'll open the door. If you reach out your hand, I'll get the elves to shake it.

The children create snowmen to ride on with the reindeer. They head to Santa's Kingdom with Ify's guidance.

EXT. SANTA'S KINGDOM - DAY

The children arrive in Santa's Kingdom and meet Ify. They learn about the history of the Chieftain Elf's banishment due to lying and sabotaging Christmas toys.

ITSY-BITSY

(to Ify)

So Santa is the Chieftain now?

IFY

No, but he stands in for the Chieftain Elf.

Ify explains the Chieftain Elf's exile to the South Pole and how the elves celebrated his departure.

ITSY-BITSY

(to Ify)

This is fascinating!

Ify shares that they celebrate Upcycle Day, where discarded toys are reconditioned to fight climate change.

ITSY-BITSY

(to the children)

Let's write our Christmas wish lists on our postcards!

The next day, the children attend the Upcycle Day Festival. There are festivities, fireworks, and preparations for Santa's arrival.

INT. SANTA'S WORKSHOP - DAY

Inside the workshop, elves are busy with the toys sent by Garden Fairies. Itsy-Bitsy spots her lost doll.

ITSY-BITSY

(excited)

There's Betsy Wetsy!

The children give Santa their postcards and receive candy canes and cookies. The Garden Fairy collects the postcards and a cookie to take back.

EXT. SANTA KINGDOM - DAY

The children slide down a metal chute with the help of Elf Ify and enjoy the festivities. Santa asks Ify to find Itsy-Bitsy's doll, and he succeeds.

ITSY-BITSY

(happy)

Thank you, Ifty! Thank you, Santa!

As the Cap Cloud approaches, the children prepare to leave. Jumping-Jack carries them back onto the cloud, and they set off into the sky.

## ACT 10 - Chain Link

Setting: Terrain Chain Link, Dense Forest, Light Ray, Archive Book


EXT. TERRAIN CHAIN LINK - DAY


The Cap Cloud descends on Terrain Chain Link, and Itsy-Bitsy prepares to meet the Terrain Chieftain Change Link.


CAP CLOUD

(voice)

Stay safe on the cloud, Itsy-Bitsy. This terrain is dangerous.


Itsy-Bitsy bravely rides Jumping-Jack to the ground and meets the Terrain Chieftain and Link Runner.


ITSY-BITSY

(curious)

I want to know the truth.

Link Runner presents the archive book and helps Itsy-Bitsy find her name, revealing her true identity.

LINK RUNNER

(points to the book)

There, Itsy-Bitsy Cloud.

The Chieftain reveals that Itsy-Bitsy was switched with a human baby and that she belongs to the Change Link Terrain.

ITSY-BITSY

(teary-eyed)

What's going to happen to me now?

The Chieftain explains that the Godmother Fairy arranged this visit so Itsy-Bitsy could know the truth and no longer live a lie. He assures her that she'll still be loved in her adopted Human World.

ITSY-BITSY

(confused)

Can I meet the girl I was switched with?

The Chieftain explains that the girl passed away after an accident. He reassures Itsy-Bitsy about her return to her human family.

ITSY-BITSY

(relieved)

I'll be returned to them?

The Chieftain tells Itsy-Bitsy to follow the terms set by the Godmother Fairy for her travels on the Clap Cloud.

ITSY-BITSY

(determined)

I will!

Itsy-Bitsy realizes that her postcard must be given to the Terrain Chieftain Change Link.

ITSY-BITSY

(to Link Runner)

Can you help me place this postcard in the book?

Itsy-Bitsy leaves her postcard on her page, and the Chieftain Link takes it as he signs the book.


GARDEN FAIRY

(from the book)

I'll take that!


The Garden Fairy emerges from the book and takes the postcard, flying away.


EXT. TREE TOP - DAY


The Cap Cloud appears above the tree, and Jumping-Jack carries Itsy-Bitsy, her doll, and her angel halo up to the cloud.


CHILDREN

(excited)

Itsy-Bitsy! You're back!


The children celebrate Itsy-Bitsy's return and nickname her the Cap Cloud Angel.

## ACT 11 - Kelpie, The Horse

Setting: Kelpie Terrain, River Bank

EXT. KELPIE TERRAIN - RIVER BANK - DAY

The Clap Cloud approaches the Kelpie Terrain slowly, and the children wake up to the sound of a distinctive horse-like call. They spot a blue horse-like creature by the river bank.

CHILD 1
(excited)
Look over there! A blue horse!

The Clap Cloud hovers near the horse, and the children take turns petting it. The horse seems friendly and appreciative of their attention.

CHILD 2
(to Jumping-Jack)
Help me up, Jumping-Jack. I want to ride the horse!

The children take turns riding the horse's back. One child gives up their space for Itsy-Bitsy. But as the children try to dismount, they find themselves stuck to the horse's back.

ITSY-BITSY
(horrified)
Oh no! What's happening?

Itsy-Bitsy rushes over and tries to pry the children off one by one using the postcards, but the postcards stick to the horse as well.

The horse gallops into the river, carrying the stuck children with it. Itsy-Bitsy watches in shock as the horse disappears into the water. She sees her own postcard floating on the water's surface.

GARDEN FAIRY
(from behind a tree)
Don't worry, Itsy-Bitsy.

The Garden Fairy dressed in blue appears and retrieves Itsy-Bitsy's postcard from the water.

ITSY-BITSY
(teary-eyed)
What happened? Where did the horse go?

The Garden Fairy flies away with the postcard, leaving Itsy-Bitsy feeling lost and alone.

EXT. CAP CLOUD - DAY

The Clap Cloud arrives, and Jumping-Jack quickly places Itsy-Bitsy and her doll onto the cloud.

ITSY-BITSY
(in tears)
I want to go home. I have no postcards left.

As the Clap Cloud carries them away, Itsy-Bitsy's emotions weigh heavy on her heart.

## ACT 12 - The Storm

Setting: Itsy-Bitsy's Bedroom

INT. ITSY-BITSY'S BEDROOM - MORNING

A storm rages outside, with rain and wind blowing fiercely. Itsy-Bitsy's bedroom window is open, and the curtains flutter in the wind. The shutters rattle, creating eerie noises.

ITSY-BITSY
(drowsy)
(mumbling)
Huh? What's that noise?

ZIGGY
(from outside the room)
(frustrated)
Itsy-Bitsy, close your window! It's a storm!

Ziggy, already awake and getting ready for school, enters Itsy-Bitsy's room and slams the window shut. Itsy-Bitsy stirs awake, disoriented.

ITSY-BITSY
(groggy)
Ziggy? What's happening?

ZIGGY
(angry)
You left your window open during a storm! The curtains were flying everywhere, and the shutters were banging like crazy!

Itsy-Bitsy blinks, realizing her mistake and the chaos caused by the storm entering her room.

ITSY-BITSY
(slightly embarrassed)
Oops... Sorry, Ziggy. I didn't realize the storm would be this strong.

ZIGGY
(annoyed)
Well, now you know! I had to come in and close the window before everything flew away!

ITSY-BITSY
(thankful)
Thanks for closing it, Ziggy.

ZIGGY
(grumpy)
Yeah, yeah. Just be more careful next time. I don't want to deal with your mess.

As Ziggy heads out of the room, Itsy-Bitsy can't help but smile at her brother's protective yet grumbling nature. The storm continues outside, but Itsy-Bitsy is safe and warm in her room.

THE END

www.ingramcontent.com/pod-product-compliance
Lightning Source LLC
LaVergne TN
LVHW041551070526
838199LV00046B/1908